SNOWFLAKES & HEARTACHES

J.M. GOODRICH

Chapter One

Everything for tomorrow is all set and ready. I have the absolute perfect wedding planned to the most perfect man I have ever met. In less than twelve hours I would become Mrs Ethan Brooks. I couldn't wait.

Christmas has always been my absolute favorite time of the year. I tend to always get a little carried away with the decorating and planning. And my wedding was no exception.

The theme of my wedding was a no-brainer. Ever since I was a little girl, I had dreamed of walking down an aisle lined with blue and silver sparkling flowers, with everything covered in fake, sparkly snowflakes. I wanted the place filled with trees that were dripping in tinsel, blue and silver ornaments, and topped with a giant, glittering snowflake.

I guess you could say I loved anything glittery, And

snowflakes. I really loved them.

Okay, it was more of a borderline obsession.

But I loved it. And Ethan, being the amazing man he was, didn't seem to mind all the glitter. "I'm just excited to start my life with you," he had told me. "This is your big day. If you want it filled with sparkles and snowflakes, you go ahead and fill it with sparkles and snowflakes. Hell," he laughed, kissing me playfully on the tip of my nose, "I'll even wear a shiny tux, looking like a walking disco ball if it means I get to marry you."

I smiled at the memory. It was one of my favorites.

God, I loved that man.

And tomorrow, in my own little private winter wonderland, I would become his wife.

I almost squealed with excitement as I hung up my wedding dress, making sure not to wrinkle it. I had searched for months for the perfect dress, and I was very protective of it.

It was a strapless gown, with a fitted notice covered in sparkles, hugging my curves in all the right places. The skirt flowed from my waist all the way to the floor, just skimming it. The bottom of the skirt had been dyed a beautiful icy blue color, with snowflakes dancing around the edge. The center of the dress was white, which faded down into the blue. I couldn't have found a more perfect dress for tomorrow. I couldn't wait to see Ethan's face when he saw me in it for the first time.

I would be carrying a bouquet of icy blue roses that

had been carefully dipped in silver glitter along the edges of their petals. The ribbon tied around the stems was white with sparkly snowflakes printed along it.

See - borderline obsessed. But I was in love with the glittery winter wonderland I had made. It was exactly how I imagined it as a kid. I have always loved weddings, and even made my own wedding idea book that I added to throughout the years. Some things may have changed over the years, but the theme always remained the same.

"You are going to be the most beautiful Snow Queen tomorrow," my mother laughed from the doorway.

"Princess," I said, "Snow Princess. 'Queen' just sounds so... old."

"Nothing wrong with being old," mother pointed out.

Smiling, I sat down beside her. "I can't believe it's finally here," I sighed, laying my head down on her shoulder. "I can't believe I am getting married in just a few short hours."

"I still can't believe my baby is all grown up," she laughed. "I hope everything is how you imagined it, sweetheart. I remember how, every winter you just... lit up. Nothing made you happier than watching the snow softly falling to the earth. I can't count the number of times I feared that you would freeze to death out there one day," she shook her head, lost in memories.

"I believed that the snow would protect me," I laughed at my younger self. "That no harm would come to me. The entire holiday season brought nothing but love, happiness, comfort, joy. The feeling of family," I squeezed my mother into a hug.

The door flew open, startling us both. Carol barely caught herself before tumbling to the floor. "Speaking of family," I laughed, watching my sister try to catch her breath and compose herself.

She glanced over at mother, and the two of them shared a look.

"What?" I asked. Neither of them said a word. Carol looked down at her feet, shifting uncomfortably. "What's going on?" I asked again, a little more forcefully this time. "Nothing's wrong, right? The flowers are all here, the cake's all set. We didn't forget anything, did we?" I began to panic a little. I reached for my planner, scanning my to-do list. I was sure everything was set and ready. That every last detail was finished.

"Sit down," mother said, taking my planner out of my hands. I reached for it but she tucked it into her purse. "That can wait."

Uh oh.

I slowly sat back down, staring at my sister. "Carol?" I asked slowly. "What is it?"

Carol looked to mother for help, but she shook her head. Closing her eyes, she let out a long breath, rubbing her head as if what she was about to tell me caused her physical pain.

I began to worry a little more.

"I just received a call from Megan," she began. Megan was one of my best friends, as well as one of my bridesmaids.

"Oh. Is she alright? She's still going to be able to make it tomorrow, right?"

"Holly," Carol shifted so she was looking me in the eye. "She's alright, she's fine. But," she hesitated, "Ethan had called her."

My heart stopped. "Why would he be calling her?"

Carol rubbed at her forehead again. "He's not coming tomorrow, Hol. I'm so sorry."

"What do you mean he's not coming tomorrow? He has to, we're getting married. He can't miss our wedding," I insisted.

She took in a shaky breath, and I knew that what she was about to tell me pained her to do so. "Over the weekend he... went away."

I nodded. "I know. He had his bachelor party. Just as I had my bachelorette party," I laughed. This was getting ridiculous.

"No, Hol," Carol shook her head, curls bouncing all over the place, "You don't understand. He didn't have a bachelor party. He went away with Jenny. They reconnected and want to give their relationship another try. He's not coming back. The wedding's off. I am so, so sorry Holly," she finished through a stream of tears.

I couldn't move. I felt like I couldn't breathe. "How did this happen?" I whispered.

"I don't know," she shrugged. "I told you all I know. I am so sorry."

"Did you know about this?" I asked my mother, who had stayed silent this whole time.

"I had my suspicions," she replied.

"And you didn't think to say anything?" I yelled, causing her to jump in her seat.

"No, I'm sorry sweetheart. I didn't want to make a fuss in case it turned out to be nothing. I was hoping it was just a case of old friends catching up. I didn't want to think the worst of Ethan. I loved him, and was looking forward to having him join our family tomorrow."

I didn't know what to think, what to do. I grabbed my phone, dialing Ethan's number. Hopefully he could shed some light on all of this. Maybe they were all mistaken. They had to be. Ethan and I were in love. It wasn't a perfect love, but it was pretty dang close.

I couldn't lose him.

But the call didn't go through. "He blocked my number," I said, as my phone slipped through my fingers and fell to the floor. "He blocked my number already. It really is over, isn't it?" I asked as I collapsed into my mother's arms.

She and Carol just exchanged silent glances as I cried my heart out. The shiny, glittery decorations that had brought me happiness all my life suddenly felt cold, dull, lifeless.

Much like myself right now.

Chapter Two

My friends attempted to comfort me, but I honestly didn't hear a single word anyone said. I just felt their hands as they tugged at me, trying to get my attention or pulling me in for a hug. I saw the looks of sympathy, sadness, anger, and worry splashed across their faces. But I couldn't feel anything.

I swear I could actually hear my shattered heart rattling around in my chest, like a million tiny shards of broken glass.

I couldn't breathe. I needed to get out of here. I started walking towards the front door when Carol stopped me, handing me a glass of wine.

"Come on," she insisted, "stay. Sit with us. We'll figure this out together." She led me back to the couches and gently guided me down onto it. The other girls silently sipped their own wine, watching me over the tops of their glasses. No doubt waiting for me to snap or explode with anger.

Problem was, I didn't feel angry. But I know I should. I didn't feel anything. Except confused.

Why?

Why did he do this? Why now? Why her? Didn't he love me? I had so many more questions. None that would get any answers though. Ethan didn't want anything to do with me, and I had no idea why.

"I think," Sara said, falling into an armchair across the room, "that what you need to do is just forget him. Wash your hands of him and move on."

I stared at her, mouth wide open. "Forget him?" I scoffed. "I spent years with that man. He was a huge part of my life. I loved him more than anything." I folded my arms stubbornly and focused my gaze on the floor. I had given him everything for so many years, every part of me. We were building a life together, and were mere hours away from tying the knot. How could I just throw that all away for good, all the memories? The heartache and betrayal I would be glad to forget and never think of again. But there were so many good times we had together. I didn't know if I could just erase it all from my life.

While I sifted through the memories of my shattered love life, the girls continued discussing what I should and shouldn't do about the situation. After a few minutes I could feel their eyes on me. Snapping out of my walk down memory lane I looked to see each of them staring directly at me, as if they were expecting an answer.

"What?" I asked.

Carol laughed. "We asked what you thought of our plan, silly."

"Uh, what plan?"

Sara shook her head while my mother tried to hide her laughter. "We decided that you should go ahead with the honeymoon," she said while the others nodded.

They can't be serious. "Why would I want to do that?"

"To get away," she shrugged.

"It could be good for you," my mother added, her tone soft yet edged with concern. "Get away from here, from certain people,' she said, rolling her eyes, "We can deal with all the difficult tasks like calling vendors and caterers and letting everyone know the wedding is off."

My heart felt like it was being squeezed right out of my chest. Now that it was said out loud, it felt that much more real. I couldn't take this anymore, I had to get out of here. Hopping out of my seat, I quickly grabbed my belongings and ran outside. As I took in deep breaths of the crisp winter air, tears began to stream down my face.

Maybe they were right, I could use some time away. I don't think I'd be able to handle the task of dismantling my wintery dream wedding.

Chapter Three

My heart jumped as the plane landed. It was a smooth landing after a calm flight, but planes still made me nervous.

I still can't believe I let everyone talk me into taking this trip.

I was in a strange city. Alone. On what was supposed to be my honeymoon.

I quickly located my luggage, which wasn't hard considering it was such a small airport, and the fact that I had sparkly snowflake-shaped luggage tags, and headed outside to call a cab. As I stepped outside I was hit by a blast of cool air. Huge fat flakes danced all around me before settling into a light dusting on the ground. I took a minute to slowly take in a deep breath, breathing in the crisp winter air.

It has always calmed me. Some people preferred the

sounds of rushing water or soothing classical music. Not me. I needed the chill of a winter's night. It was magic to me.

My head now cleared, I took out my phone and called a cab to take me to the Inn.

"Where ya headed?" The driver asked as I hopped in, brushing snow off my shoulders and out of my eyes.

"The Christmas Inn." I answered. The name itself was perfect. From the pictures I saw online it would be cozy, warm, and just like Christmas at home with my family. I couldn't wait.

As we drove to the Inn I stared out the window at the scenery before me. The entire town was covered in Christmas lights and decorations. The Holiday spirit was in full swing here.

Maybe this wouldn't be so bad after all, I thought.

Each streetlight we passed had garland wound up its pole, and at the top sat either a wreath or a giant sized ornament. The window shops each held their own miniature winter scene. I was already looking forward to walking down the street and taking a closer look at each one.

A tear slid down my cheek at the thought of having to do it all alone. I was supposed to be doing this with my new husband. Walking down the street, arm in arm as we looked at Christmas decorations had been one of the many things I had been looking forward to on this trip. Christmas is such a magical time, and you're supposed to be sharing it with the ones you love.

I was supposed to be married by now. My heart sank in my chest. I didn't want to miss Ethan. I really didn't. I should be hating him for what he did to me. For ripping out my heart and stomping on it. Hating him for trying to ruin my favorite season.

"We're here," the driver announced. I let out a long sigh. I had been so busy feeling sorry for myself that I hadn't even noticed where we were.

I stepped out of the cab and took in the sight of the Inn. Icicle lights were everywhere, and a giant inflatable Santa with his sleight sat proudly in the front yard. Two towering trees stood, one on each side of the entrance to the Inn. Both of them were fully decked out in decorations and absolutely breathtaking. I handed the driver the money owed to him, grabbed my bags, and walked up the steps, a huge smile plastered on my face.

"Well hello there, Merry Christmas," a woman said cheerfully from behind the front desk.

"Hi," I answered back as I set my luggage down at my feet.

"How may I help you?" she asked.

"I am checking in."

The cheerful woman clapped her hands together. "Excellent. May I have your name please?" she asked, placing her hands on her keyboard.

"Holly. Holly Walker. Or maybe Brooks," I added

with a nervous laugh. "I'm not sure which one. See, I was supposed to be here on my honeymoon, but the wedding ... never happened. So I'm here. Alone." And rambling. How embarrassing. I shut up when the woman gave me a sympathetic smile, turning back to the computer screen in front of her.

She blew out a breath. "I'm sorry, dear. It looks like we gave your room away."

"You ... what?" I stammered.

"I'm so sorry," she shook her head slowly. Pushing back her glasses she said, "It looks like an Ethan Brooks called here last week to cancel the reservation. He didn't tell you?" She turned to me.

"No, he only broke off our wedding two days ago..." I trailed off.

"Oh, dear."

It didn't make sense. How could he have called to cancel our room before he even ran into his ex - whatever her name was. It wasn't important. Had he been seeing her behind my back? Or did he just not love me anymore? Either way, it hurt like hell.

"Is there possibly another room that I could get?" I asked in a voice that was barely above a whisper.

"I'm so sorry dear. With the holidays so close, we're booked up solid. So is everyone else in town, I'm afraid."

Wonderful. "Oh, okay," I answered. "Thank you."

"Merry Christmas," she offered.

I mumbled something under my breath and grabbed

my bags, heading back out into the cold. I stood at the side of the road, not knowing what to do or where to go from here. Everything was quickly crashing down around me.

The crisp air and snowflakes falling all around me were no longer charming. I was cold. And angry.

Not knowing what else to do, I began dragging my luggage down the snowy street, past carolers and people shopping for last minute gifts. Past bakeries that gave off the smell of freshly baked cookies and bread.

"How could this possibly get any worse?" I cried out loud, sinking down onto a nearby bench. As I did, some of the snow from the streetlight above me fell both on top of my head and straight down the back of jacket and shirt, causing me to shiver. I cursed under my breath.

I couldn't hold it in any longer, tears started streaming hot and fast down my face. This wasn't at all how this trip was supposed to go. Everything was wrong. I shouldn't have listened to Carol. I shouldn't have come here.

"Excuse me, are you alright?"

I sniffed and looked up, wiping wet snowflakes off my eyelashes. Before me stood a man. "I, uh..." I blinked hard a few times, fearing I'd stared too long at him. "I've been better," I admitted, my shoulders slumping in defeat.

The man looked around. "Do you need anything? Any assistance? You're not here alone, are you?" He asked, eyeing my luggage laying haphazardly in the snow at my feet.

I knew you shouldn't talk to strangers and you really shouldn't admit to them that you happen to be alone in a strange town, but I was desperate. Not to mention freezing.

"I am. I wasn't supposed to be," I sniffed. "I'm actually supposed to be on my honeymoon right now. But the wedding didn't happen because the bastard left me at the last minute to get back together with his ex. But I came here anyway, only to find out that my room was given away. I don't know anyone here, or my way around, or... "Once again, I was rambling. A nervous habit I've always had. Once I started it was almost impossible to get me to shut up.

The gentleman, seeming unfazed by the fact that I just unloaded on a complete stranger, brushed the snow off the bench and sat down beside me.

I sniffed again, wiping my nose on my glove. Attractive, I know. "I'm sorry," I said as I took in a shaky breath. "It has just been a long, unhappy day." I turned to look at the man seated next to me. I opened my mouth to say something else but stopped when I saw just how handsome he was.

He smiled at me. "Don't be. I'm Gabe, by the way. Gabe Winters."

"Holly," I replied. "Are you from around here?"

"As a matter of fact, I am. My family and I own an

Inn just up the street here," he said, nodding to our right. "We always keep a room open for emergencies, such as yours," he gave a soft laugh. "It's yours if you're interested."

"Seriously?" I asked, perking up for the first time in days. "You would do that for me?"

Gabe stood up. "Of course. From the sound of it you've had a rough few days. And everyone else in town is full. Besides," he said, bending down to pick up my bags for me, "no one should be alone on Christmas. So what do you say?"

I smiled up at him, his eyes twinkling in the lights. "It sounds like the best news I've had in days," I laughed. "Are you sure your family won't mind?"

"Are you kidding?" Gabe laughed. "My family is all about Christmas. We live for it. My mom always says - the more, the merrier."

"I love Christmas too. It has always been my absolute favorite time of year. But this year..." I sighed, trailing off.

"Not so much?" Gabe asked softly.

I nodded. "Not so much."

"That's too bad. Perhaps we can change that. Come on," he said, "the Inn is just a short walk from here."

We walked side by side in silence for a few minutes before he gestured to my bags. "So I see you like snowflakes,"

I laughed. If he only knew. I had little snowflakes everywhere, all year round. On my luggage tags, cell phone case, keychains, earrings, decals on my laptop, everywhere. "I sure do. I think they're beautiful," I admitted. "And unique. The sparklier, the better too." I added.

"Well," Gabe said, "our Inn is called the Snowfall Inn. I know it's not 'snowflake' but it's pretty darn close," he laughed as he stopped in front of a large building. "Speaking of, we're here."

Chapter Four

The front of the Snowfall Inn had plastic reindeer and Santa's sleigh on the front lawn, icicle lights dangled off the roof, casting the Inn in a dreamy light blue haze. Each tree on the lawn was decorated with its own theme and color scheme. The walkway leading up to the front door was decorated along the sides with giant lights in the shape of Christmas bulbs. It was a magical sight.

Gabe slowly led me to the front door, letting me take in the colorful scene. "You ready?" he asked as we stood in front of the door. Covering just about half of the door was a large wreath made out of silver and blue bells. We had one like it growing up back home. Only ours was much smaller of course.

I nodded nervously. Gabe placed his hand on the knob and pushed open the door. My mouth fell open at the sight. The outside was nothing compared to the magic that awaited us inside. I was not prepared for what laid on the other side of that door. You were hit with Christmas charm and spirit before even taking a single step inside the Inn.

"Welcome to the Snowfall Inn," Gabe announced proudly.

I stepped inside as he closed the door behind me. The air was scented with peppermint, vanilla, and a hint of orange and cinnamon. It was warm and inviting.

Directly in front of us was a staircase leading up to the second floor. Garland with lights was wrapped around the banister leading the entire way up. In between each slat hung a shiny bulb.

"All the guest rooms are up there," Gabe nodded, following my gaze. "Now, would you like to see your room, or would you like a tour of the place first?" he asked with a smile.

"Tour, please." I bounced on the balls of my feet with excitement. I took off my jacket and scarf, handing them both to Gabe. As he hung them up in the front closet I stole a quick look around. I noticed festive bells hanging on each doorknob. And in every corner there stood a mini tree, each decorated in a separate color. Similar to those out on the lawn.

"Ready?" Gabe led me to the room to the right of the stairs. "Now, our Inn isn't the largest, but in my opinion, we're the best Inn, also the friendliest," he winked, making me laugh.

"Here, we have the dining room," Gabe said, gesturing to the large table in the center of the room. It was long enough to seat twenty people, at least. Each place setting had its own woven placemat, decorated with its own individual winter scene. A silver table runner trimmed in gold laid across the table. Along the center of the table runner sat glass candleholders in the shape of snowflakes. I practically squealed when I noticed them.

Gabe just raised an eyebrow at me and smirked.

"What?" I laughed. "I love snowflakes, I can't help it," I said, bobbing my shoulders up and down. Gabe shook his head in amusement, continuing with the tour.

"Every night at 7pm we hold a big, family-style dinner. My mother makes the most amazing food. Although, I may be biased," he winked. "You aren't obligated to sit and eat with us, but you are more than welcome to."

A home cooked meal each night did sound great. "Thanks," I said. "I think I'd like that." I genuinely meant it. Sharing a big family meal was something I always looked forward to, especially during the holidays. Good food and lively chatter, what could be better?

"In here is the kitchen,' Gabe said, leading me into the next room. As I walked through the doorway I passed by two wooden nutcrackers standing guard. They stood about three feet tall. One held a small tray of cookies while the other held a tray of brownies.

"Go ahead," he told me. I shot him a confused look, and he laughed. "The treats on their trays are real."

"They sure are. Fresh too," a woman said, approaching us. She wiped her flour covered hands on a towel before pulling Gabe in for a hug. "How are you, my dear?" she asked him.

"Never better, mom," he beamed.

Mom? Looking closer, they did look a lot alike. They shared the same piercing blue eyes and warm smiles.

"That's what I want to hear. Now, who have we got here?" she asked, turning her attention to me. She had such a welcoming feeling about her.

Gabe stepped next to me, and, putting his arm around me, told her "This is Holly. She's here for a ... vacation," he said, shooting me a quick glance, "and her room at another Inn was given away before she had even gotten there. I thought she could stay in the room we set aside for occasions such as this," he said, giving my shoulders a little shake. I was glad he answered for me. I had a mouthful of brownie when his mother showed up.

I quickly swallowed the brownie - man, it was good - and held out of my hand. "It's a pleasure to meet you, Mrs Winters. And thank you so much for taking me in at the last minute. I can't tell you how much I appreciate it. These brownies are amazing, by the way." I added.

Gabe laughed. "She's a nervous rambler," he explained with a wink.

"Well, then," Mrs Winters laughed, taking my hands in hers, "First, you may call me Mary if you'd like. We're all like family here at the Snowfall Inn," she said with a twinkle in her eyes.

"Thank you."

"After you finish the tour and are settled in your room, you are more than welcome to come down and mingle," Mary laughed again. "There's hot cocoa and cookies by the fire every evening. It's a nice time to unwind from the day, and get to meet some new friends." She nudged Gabe on the shoulder, which made him roll his eyes.

"That sounds lovely," I admitted. Sitting by the fireside with a steaming mug of cocoa was always what I looked forward to after spending the day out in the blustery cold.

Gabe and I continued on with the tour. He showed me where all the snacks were in case I was hungry in the middle of the night, where the extra towels were, and anything else I might need during my stay.

This whole Inn was magical. Mistletoe hung in almost every doorway. I was careful to avoid being caught underneath it.

Every room you looked at, there was a medium sized tree in every corner, each with its own theme. Twinkly lights and garland were strung along the walls, lining each room. Every door knob had its own set of bells dangling from it.

Gabe stopped in front of me. "Before I show you the living room, I'd like to take you upstairs."

I narrowed my eyes at him. "Excuse me?"

He looked at me, confused for a second, then burst out with laughter. "Oh my, not like that," he said, "I meant to show you your room first." He wiped a tear from his eyes. It was kind of cute. "The living room is my favorite part of the Inn. It's where we all gather, share stories and memories, share in the magic of Christmas." His eyes twinkled. "You'll see when we get there."

A huge smile spread across my lips. It was nice to finally meet someone who loved this season as much as I did. I had been afraid that I would be stuck with a bunch of weirdos here. Or worse - couples on their honeymoon and being all lovey-dovey.

The upstairs was where all the guest rooms were located. Set up against the railing was the most detailed miniature Christmas village I have ever seen. Tiny houses and businesses decorated with twinkling lights. Tiny people twirling in circles as they danced on the ice. I could look at it for hours.

"Here's your room," Gabe announced cheerfully. I tore my attention away from the village. I could always come back to look at it later. He was standing in front of the door to the left of the stairs.

Gabe opened the door and I gasped. It was like

walking into my own little Christmas world. Lights and garland were strung over each window, a blue and silver comforter on the bed, with a sparkling wreath hanging on the wall above the headboard.

In the corner of the room was a table with a miniature tree on top of it, complete with decorations.

"I thought you'd want to see these," Gabe said. He walked over to the window, pulling aside the curtains to reveal window clings in the shape of sparkly snowflakes.

My eyes lit up. "They're on all the windows, all over the Inn," Gabe laughed.

I practically squealed. "I love it. I love the whole Inn so far," I admitted. I turned to face Gabe. "Thank you again, so much, for letting me stay here. I seriously don't know what I would have done if you hadn't come along and rescued me."

The smile on Gabe's face made my heart skip a beat. No man should ever look that good. "It's my pleasure, really," he said. "Helping people is what Christmas is all about."

"So," he said, clapping his hands together, "are you ready for the main event?"

"Absolutely," I beamed, as he led m e back downstairs.

"Everyone usually spends most of their time here at the Inn gathered in the living room," Gabe said. "You can sit by the fire, curl up with a good book. We have a shelf full right over there," he pointed to the wall opposite the fireplace. "You don't have to sit and talk with people if you don't want to. All the other guests are pretty understanding and will leave you alone if you wish," he said, laughing to himself. "It's just a nice place to sit, relax, and soak in all the holiday spirit.

"And here we are," Gabe said proudly, sweeping his hands across the room.

My mouth fell open at the magical sight before me. Every inch of the room was decorated and twinkling, either with lights or glitter. Above the roaring fireplace hung a row of stockings, each with the word 'Guest' stitched across it. Above those on the mantle was thick fragrant greenery with several candles in red glass candleholders.

In each corner stood either a giant nutcracker or soldier, again holding trays of freshly baked treats.

It was beautiful. The one thing that stood out and seemed odd to me was the tree. Standing tall next to the fireplace was one of the largest trees I've ever seen.

But it was bare. Not one single ornament was hung on its branches. No tinsel or lights. No star or angel sitting up on the top. I shot Gabe a confused look.

He chuckled. "There's a reason for that, I promise," he said as he led me closer. "We have a tradition here at the Snowfall Inn. Well, we have many of them," he laughed, "But every Christmas Eve all the guests gather and decorate the tree together. We usually do it in the morning. Some guests even make an ornament to add every year. But it's not something that's required," he winked.

"Oh good, you're telling Holly about our traditions." I turned to see Mrs. Winters standing behind us, a huge smile plastered across her face. "It's my favorite part," she added.

"Mine too," Gabe said as he continued. "After the tree is decorated and all lit up, cocoa and sugar cookies are passed around ..."

"All homemade," Mary laughed.

"All homemade, yes," he smiled, "and we write Christmas cards and wrap presents."

Sounds like your typical Christmas Eve. Only with a lot more people.

"Then we bring the gifts down to the children's orphanage and hand them out. We try to make sure each child gets at least one pair of warm clothing, a sweet treat, and a couple small toys to play with. The looks on their faces as they open up their gifts is my absolute favorite part of Christmas."

I looked at Gabe, tears pricking at my eyes. Spending the holidays giving back to the less fortunate was something Ethan would never have done. He was always a little ... selfish. Gabe was the complete opposite.

I couldn't think of a better way to spend the day. "I can't wait to do all that," I admitted. "It sounds like a wonderful day."

"It truly is," Mary said as she wrapped her arms

around me again. "I'm so glad you're going to join us this year."

"Me too," I replied, patting her arms. And with that my entire mood was lifted. I couldn't wait to be a part of their heartwarming tradition.

Chapter Five

Besides me, there were four other guests staying at the Inn. The first was an older couple, Betty and George St. James, that came to spend every Christmas Eve and Christmas here at the Inn. They first stayed here for their honeymoon and loved it so much, they booked the same room year after year. How cute is that? I had been looking forward to starting traditions like that of my own with Ethan.

I have got to stop thinking about him.

The other guests were a single mother, Tina Crawford, and her only daughter, Desiree. She was six years old and the cutest little thing. When we were being introduced, she ran over to me and threw her arms around my legs for a hug. She then looked up at me, telling me that I was pretty and that I should call her Desi. The other guests laughed as Tina attempted to pull her off me, looking embarrassed, but I told her not to worry. I loved kids. Someday I hoped to have a couple of my own.

The limited number of guests made being here on my own, suddenly not that bad. Everyone had been so warm and friendly towards me since the minute Gabe found me sitting in the snow. Hopefully I wouldn't bring down the mood at all with my sob story. Not that I planned on going around talking about it. But one look around this room told me that I wouldn't have much time to be sad. The Christmas Spirit was everywhere here, alive and well.

This trip was the right idea after all.

After chatting with everyone and sharing stories for a few hours, the others started making their way up to their rooms for the night. I wasn't all that tired yet so I chose to stay behind, curling up in one of the fluffy armchairs next to the roaring fire.

I was staring into the flames, trying not to think about how I was supposed to be on my honeymoon right now. I was lost in my thoughts, and hadn't noticed that Mary was standing right next to me.

"How are you doing, dear?" She asked, causing me to jump. I put my hand on my chest to calm my beating heart. "Oh my, I didn't mean to startle you."

"It's alright," I assured her, straightening up in the chair. "I must have been daydreaming."

She chuckled and held out a mug. "I thought you could use this."

I took the mug and inhaled the scent. "This smells amazing." It tasted even better. It was a rich hot chocolate, topped with a sweet whipped cream that had crushed Andes mints sprinkled on the top. It was pure heaven in a mug.

"It's an old family recipe," she said proudly, taking a seat in the chair opposite me. "But really, how are you? Are you holding up okay? I heard bits and pieces of what had happened to you. That's such a terrible thing to have to go through. Especially at Christmas time."

I wrapped my hands around the mug, the warmth comforting me. "I will admit, I have been better." She nodded in understanding. I hadn't meant to tell everyone what happened, with them being strangers and all, but it just slipped out. Earlier, when all the guests were gathered around in the living room telling stories, it just felt safe. Like I could talk to them about anything and no one would judge, or make snarky comments or anything like that. The Winters had created a safe, loving, and welcoming environment here at the Snowfall Inn.

Shaking my head, I tell her, "But I'll be alright. I'm just trying to get through the holidays."

Mary walked over to me and took my hand in hers. "You don't have to just 'get through the holidays.' Everyone here, even though we are still practically strangers to you, we are here for you. Even if it's just a shoulder to lean on, or someone to listen to whatever you need to say. Everyone who stays at the Snowfall Inn is considered family. We've all fallen on hard times at one point in our lives. But here, we are all equal. We do what we can to make everyone feel happy and loved."

She smiled at me sweetly. I swallowed the lump in my throat that threatened to dissolve into tears. "Thank you," I said in a voice barely above a whisper. If I said anything else right now I probably would have burst into tears.

"You are more than welcome, my dear," she chuckled again as she patted my hand. She started off back towards the kitchen when she stopped, turning her head back my way. "I hope the rest of your stay is a happier one. I know Gabe sure is happy you are here." She winked before turning back and disappearing around the corner.

I didn't even want to pretend to know what she meant by that comment. I shook my head and raised the still steaming mug to my lips, taking a sip of the sweet cocoa. This seriously was the best cup of hot cocoa I have ever had. I wonder what I'd have to do to get a copy of the recipe from Mary?

Chapter Six

I woke up on my third day here, feeling more at home than I ever had in my real one. Mary and Nicholas had gone above and beyond to make every one of us feel special. They poured their heart and soul into everything they did.

Betty and George were designated the Inn's unofficial grandparents, and you could tell they loved the idea. Betty had a purse full of candy and she was always shoving one in your hand. George would sit by the fire and both tell stories that entertained everyone or would take random objects, whatever he could find, and invent some sort of game out of them. Because of that, you could always find Desi right by his side. Tina didn't seem to mind the small break she got from that, either.

Tina and Desi were like the sister and niece that I

never had. Yes, I have an actual sister. But Carol and I didn't bond the way Tina and I did. Don't get me wrong, I love my sister. Sometimes she just got so wrapped up in her own life that I wouldn't hear from her for months on end. Tina had taken me out and shown me a little of the town one day while Desi was caught up in a new game with George. We went shopping, looking at Christmas decorations, and found a really good pastry shop. I wish Carol and I would have had more days like this. Or any days like this, really.

I was staring out the window, enjoying one of the delicious blueberry muffins Mary makes each morning when I felt someone tug on the bottom of my shirt. I looked down to see Desi smiling up at me.

"Miss Holly, will you go outside and have a snowball fight with me?"

"A snowball fight?"

"Yea!" She began jumping up and down. "Mommy doesn't like it when I throw snowballs at her. But it's so fun. Please?"

I laughed at how excited she was. I remember as a child spending hours out in the snow, building forts with my friends, sledding, building snowmen, and even having snowball fights with the neighborhood. We would stay out until it was dark out, which doesn't take very long in the winter, and our noses and cheeks were all red. "You know what?" I bent down to look Desi in her cute little face. "I would love to. As long as your mom says it's okay."

Her eyes grew wide. "Really?"

"Really?" I nodded. And with that she was off to get her mom's permission.

Gabe wandered down the stairs and headed straight towards me. "Morning," he smiled. "How did you sleep?"

He asked me this every morning. I wanted to feel special, but I'm sure he asked all the guests that to be polite. Still... "I slept great, thank you."

He nodded. "Any plans for the day?"

"Well," I started, when Desi came bounding back down the stairs.

"Mom says it's okay!" She said, her face glowing with excitement.

Turning to Gabe I told him, "Desi and I are going out to have a snowball fight."

"Yea, wanna come?" She asked him.

"You bet," he told her. He then turned to me. "I mean, as long as you don't mind me tagging along."

I didn't, although I wasn't sure I wanted him to see me playing in the snow and acting like a child. At least we would get to spend some time together, I suppose. "Not at all," I told him. "The more the merrier."

So the three of us spent the morning dodging snowballs and even making an army of snowmen. By lunchtime we had the entire front yard of the Inn covered with snowmen of all shapes and sizes. We didn't have enough hats and scarves to clothe them but Mary did offer us some spray bottles filled with water and food coloring, so our snowmen at least had some color to them. It looked like a rainbow out here.

"I'm getting cold," Desi said as she sprayed the last snowman with a bit of red, giving it a painted on scarf. "I'm going to go in and find my mom. Maybe she'll let me have some hot cocoa by the fire."

"I bet she will," I laughed. "I think every snow man and woman is finished," I said, looking around at our progress. Not one single snowball was left without color on it.

"I like it," Gabe commented.

"Well, I love it," Desi beamed. "Thank you for playing with me today."

Gabe bent down to her level. "It was our pleasure. I had a lot of fun today."

Desi smiled brightly before running back into the Inn to find her mother. I began to pick up the empty spray bottles, placing them back in their box. "This is the last one," I said, dropping it in with the others.

"Nope, missed one," Gabe said. I turned around to grab it from him but instead was hit in the shoulder with a snowball. I looked up to see Gabe grinning at me, half hiding behind a tree.

"Oh, it's on," I laughed, chasing him around the yard. He was too fast for me, weaving in and out of the army we created on the front lawn. I ended up slipping on a patch of ice landing on my back. "Alright, I give up," I laughed. "You win."

Gabe walked over to help me up. He grabbed my hand, carefully pulling me to my feet. As I steadied myself I noticed how close we were. I could feel the butterflies in my stomach at how close he was standing to me. My breath started coming faster.

Gabe took a step closer, never letting go of my hand. With his free hand he gently cupped the side of my face. Without hesitating he pulled my face towards his, and the world seemed to stop as his lips touched mine.

I forgot all about my pain, my heartache. It was just me, Gabe, and this moment between us as the snow began to softly fall. Big, fat flakes filled the air, adding to the magic of it all.

"Come on," he said. "Let's go."

"Go where?" I ask, a little breathless.

"The tree lighting is soon at the town square. Everyone will be there. I thought it would be nice to go for a walk, just the two of us, before we get together with everyone."

"I like that idea," I smile, taking his hand in mine. We continued walking, hand in hand, for the next couple hours as we made our way through town, admiring all the decorations on both the shops and private houses. People really loved Christmas in this town, and it showed. Everywhere I looked was a mini winter wonderland, with twinkling lights and bright, cheerful decorations. I never wanted to leave.

Before heading to the tree lighting we stopped in to get some hot cocoa. The owners of the bakery handed out snowmen cookies to anyone who stopped by.

"You gonna eat that or stare at it all night?" Gabe laughed, biting the head off his cookie.

I shook my head. "I'm going to eat it. It smells amazing. It just reminded me of how great today has been. And I have you to thank for that." I looked down at the floor, feeling my cheeks burn.

Gabe slid his chair closer to me. "I can't take all the credit for that. But I'm glad you're happy." He leaned over, planting a kiss on the top of my head. My cheeks burned hotter.

"But wait," I said between bites. "Today's only December 23rd."

Gabe nodded.

"Isn't tree lighting usually on Christmas Eve or something like that?"

"Usually, yea. But since most people prefer to hang out at home and be with their family and loved ones on that day, the town decided to do it a day earlier, so that the whole town could get together for it. Not sure if you've noticed, but everyone in town is pretty close. We're like one giant, crazy family," he winked.

"I did notice that." And I loved it. I loved everything about this town. I tried not to think about the fact that soon, I'd be back on a plane heading for home. It was strange, but this place felt more like home than my real home did.

We finished our treats and headed back out into the snow to meet up with the rest of the Inn's guests. We spotted them fairly quickly as Desi started yelling out our names the second she saw us. We walked over and Mary handed us a blanket. "Brought enough for everyone to share," she said. "It can surely get cold waiting on the tree to be lit. But it sure is beautiful." Her eyes twinkled.

"Not nearly as beautiful as you dear," Nicholas said, putting his arm around his wife.

Mary playfully hit his arm. "Oh, you," she giggled. He just laughed and pulled her closer to him. They were so cute. That was the type of love I was hoping to find someday. The type that lasts.

"Stand next to me!' Desi tugged on my jacket. I laughed and moved to stand next to her and Tina, Gabe following close behind.

"I never did thank the two of you for watching her earlier," she said. "I really appreciated it."

"Oh, it was absolutely no problem," I admitted. "We had a lot of fun."

"The Inn is now well guarded with that army you

made out front," Nicholas laughed. "I've never seen so many snowmen in one place."

Desi looked proud of herself.

I shivered as the countdown to the lighting began. The temperature had dropped a few degrees. Wordlessly, Gabe unfolded the blanket his mother had handed him. He moved right next to me, draping the blanket over both our shoulders. We huddled together under the blanket and the warmth, as everyone in the town counted down together. The tree was lit, and it sparkled with many different colors. A large star sat on the top of the tree, and it shone brilliantly. It was the biggest and brightest Christmas tree I had ever seen. Everyone clapped and cheered, the Christmas spirit thick in the air.

Cider was passed out with more snowmen cookies. Everyone drank their cider to warm up and talked excitedly with fellow townspeople about their plans for the next few days. Once the snow began falling harder everyone said their goodbyes and made their way to their homes.

We all walked back to the Inn as a group. As we walked back, still wrapped up in our blanket, I couldn't help the huge smile that was stuck on my face. Being with everyone like this, especially with Gabe, made me so happy. Happier than I've been in a while.

But, was it too soon? Am I allowed to feel this way? To be happy with another man? All of a sudden I didn't know what to think. How to feel.

This wasn't fair.

Maybe I was just scared. What I was feeling for Gabe came on fast and strong. And I was leaving in a few days.

Maybe I should just not worry so much and let things happen. Not put so much pressure on it. Just let go and enjoy my time here, whatever happens.

Why was this so confusing?

Chapter Seven

I awoke to the scent of crispy bacon and sweet french toast in the air. My mouth watered as I got dressed and headed downstairs.

A cheerful chorus of "Good morning" greeted me as I made my way into the dining room. It seems I was the last one to wake up. All of the other guests were already wide awake and seated around the table eating.

"I'm sorry we didn't wait for you," Tina said around a mouthful of food.

"Yeah, you took forever," Desi added, reaching for what looked like a second handful of bacon.

"Oh, it's alright," I laughed. "I guess I was just extra sleepy this morning." Gabe came out of the kitchen carrying a pitcher of freshly squeezed orange juice and our eyes locked as he set it down in the middle of the table. Heat rushed to my cheeks. I took a seat in the only available chair, which just happened to be right next to where Gabe was sitting. I briefly wondered if that was on purpose.

We all ate our fill of the absolutely delicious food Mary and Nick had prepared as everyone talked about how excited they were for Christmas. Especially Desi. Her little eyes lit up brightly as she talked about all the things she wanted to do as well as the gifts she hoped Santa would bring her. I couldn't help but smile at her innocence. I missed those days.

I stayed silent for most of the morning, listening to everyone's excitement. I felt a small pang of jealousy. This Christmas was so much different than I had expected. Not at all how I had pictured it would be.

I didn't want to feel this way. I know I shouldn't be feeling like this. Not after everything these wonderful people had done for me. They took me in, literally from the streets. Sharing their love and traditions with us, some who were complete strangers, and treated us like family.

This is exactly how Christmas should be.

As soon as everyone had finished eating and the dirty dishes were cleared from the table, Gabe stood up, clearing his throat. "I'm sure by now you've all noticed the bare tree sitting in the living room." Everyone nodded. "Another tradition we have here at the Snowfall Inn is letting all the guests, if they would like, decorate the tree together. Like one big family," he said, echoing my earlier thoughts. Mary beamed from her seat. You could just tell how important family was to her. And I loved how they included everyone in that. It didn't matter who you were or your background or anything. If you were a guest here at the Snowfall Inn, you were automatically considered family.

"Along with a few boxes filled with some of my favorite ornaments," Gabe continued, "we do have some art supplies for anyone who would like to make their own ornament to add their own personal touch to the tree."

Desi grabbed her mother's hand and they raced to the boxes, digging out different colored construction paper, glitter, stick-on gems, and markers. I decided to join them. "I'm going to make some snowmen, just like the ones we made out front," she exclaimed proudly.

"That's a great idea," I told her.

"What about you?"

I thought about it for a minute. "I think I'll make my own sparkly snowflakes. They're really my thing," I shrugged.

"I have seen a few of them on your belongings," Tina laughed. "I thought it was just a seasonal thing."

I shook my head, laughing. "Nope. It's an all year thing for me. I've always loved Christmas more than anything. And snowflakes are the biggest reminder of that for me. I make sure to always carry at least one around with me."

Everyone ended up making their own ornaments this year. The tree was beautifully decorated with everyone's memories. Nicholas set up his camera with a timer on it and we all posed cheerfully in front of our newly decorated tree. After making sure it looked perfect, he raced off to make copies for everyone to take home.

"Alright everyone, if I may have your attention once more," Gabe announced loudly. We all stopped what we were doing to look at him. He had the biggest smile on his face. "Now it is time for my truly favorite part of the season. The tree here is a close second," he laughed as he gestured to the memory-filled tree. "But what I love most of all, is giving. Putting a smile on someone's face and filling their heart with even a little bit of joy." His eyes landed on mine as he said that, and his gaze lingered a moment. I could feel the heat beginning to creep up. I could just blame it on standing too close to the fireplace though if anyone caught it.

Gabe continued. "All throughout the year we collect gifts, whether gently used or brand new. We store them here at the Inn until tonight. Together, we are going to wrap those gifts and bring them down to the orphanage. We give them a little party and they get to open the gifts."

Nicholas stood up and walked over to stand next to his son. "Gabe here was the one who started this whole tradition," he stated proudly, putting his arm across his shoulders. "This is a good man, here. Heart of pure gold. I know I tell you all the time, but I am so proud to call you my son," he said to Gabe as we all clapped. Mary wiped the tears from her eyes.

The more I learned about Gabe, the more I admired him.

And the harder I fell for him.

Gabe and his parents disappeared into the back room, returning a few minutes later with huge bags and boxes filled with all kinds of toys and games, wrapping paper and ribbons. Mary also brought out tray after tray of freshly baked goods for us to snack on while we wrapped the gifts. I honestly had no idea where she found the time to do all this baking and cooking. I was certainly glad she did though.

Along with the gifts were little cards where we could write an inspirational message or just a simple holiday greeting if we wished. Desi spent most of her time writing out little sayings and drawing pictures. I'm sure they would be appreciated.

Once everything was all wrapped and the cards finished, we all got on our winter gear as Gabe disappeared outside. I was walking back down the stairs from my room when I heard the sounds of horses.

"Come on," Desi poked her head in from the front door. "You have to see this!"

"Look!" She bounced up and down excitedly as she pointed to the huge red sleigh in front of me. It was pulled by two horses. The man driving the sleigh was dressed up, complete with tails on his suit and a top hat. I laughed as Gabe came from around the corner, dressed up like Santa.

"How do I look?" He twirled in a circle, a huge smile plastered on his face."

"Too skinny to be Santa," Desi laughed.

"Well, I think he looks great," I said. And I meant it. Santa was not meant to be that sexy looking though. I blushed a little, even though no one could hear my thoughts.

"The kids love it," Gabe said. "They also love that," he nodded towards his parents coming out the door. They were both dressed as Santa and Mrs Clause. The look suited Nicholas much better though. He even had a full white beard and twinkle in his eye to complete the look.

"And these," Gabe pulled a box out from under the seat, " are for all of you to wear." He pulled out one of the elf hats, complete with fake elf ears sewn onto it, and placed it on my head. "Beautiful," he winked. I rolled my eyes at him.

"What about me?" Desi asked, replacing her own hat with an elf one.

"Best looking elf I have ever seen," he told her. She giggled and walked over to pet the horses.

"This is all so amazing," I said to Gabe. "I can't believe you do this every year."

"You haven't seen anything yet," he laughed. "Just wait til you see the smile on these kids' faces. It's the most amazing feeling in the world. And not only that," he leaned a little closer. I could feel the warmth coming off him. "We also collect money for the orphanage to help out with the rest of the year. That part we don't announce to everyone," he shrugged. "Just feels like a weird thing to brag about. We just give the kids a party and celebrate with them."

"Well I think it's all just so amazing. So are you," I admitted, the last part barely coming out above a whisper.

We loaded the wrapped gifts into the sleigh and headed off through town to the orphanage. There was just enough room on the sleigh for Desi to ride. She said it made her feel like a Christmas Princess riding up there. The rest of us followed closely behind on foot.

It wasn't long before we made it to our destination. The children came out to see the sleigh being pulled by the horses and the looks on their faces was pure joy. They were so happy just seeing such a magical sight. They were able to carefully pet the horses and even take turns sitting on the sleigh with Desi. Her face lit up as she talked about her ride over here.

As they were all distracted by the sleigh, Gabe gathered a few of the adults to step inside and help set up some decorations that he had made to surprise them.

Everything this man did lately made my heart go wild. He was so thoughtful and caring and unlike any man I've ever met.

We finished setting up just as everyone started making their way inside to warm up from the cold. Kids sprinted everywhere to check out all the decorations.

"Alright everyone," Gabe clapped his hands together, demanding everyone's attention. "Who's ready to meet Santa?" With that the children began jumping up and down, squealing with excitement. He gestured for everyone to be quiet. Once they were settled down he put his hand to his ear. "I bet if we listen carefully we'll be able to hear him."

All the kids strained their little ears, trying to hear the jolly man in red coming to see them. Sure enough, after a few seconds we could hear the sound of boots stomping down the hall towards us. I smiled as Nicholas, followed by Mary, came into sight. "Ho, ho, ho," he bellowed in a low voice. "I hear there are some good little boys and girls here. Is this right?"

He was greeted by a chorus of 'Yes!' from each and every kid.

Nicholas chuckled. "Well, with the help of my elves here," he gestured to us, "I have a little gift for each of you. How does that sound?" The squeals were even louder.

We all grabbed the gifts and the cards and handed them out to each child. Every one of them thanked us as they opened their gift and ran to show them off to their friends. There were a lot of extras, so that everyone would have more than one thing to play with. There was also a bunch of clothes and blankets as well as other necessities thrown in there.

We all laughed and shared stories, ate and drank the wonderful treats that Mary had baked sometime. Seriously, that woman was a baking superwoman. I don't know how she did it.

As we were leaving I looked over to see a little girl talking with Gabe. She gave him a quick hug and when he hugged her back my heart practically melted.

"What are you smiling about?" Tina asked, nudging me in the shoulder.

I quickly shook my head, clearing my throat. "Nothing," I lied. "Well, this entire night really, I suppose. Seeing those kids so happy and having a great time was kind of magical."

"It really does get you right in the Christmas spirit, doesn't it?" She laughed, and I nodded in agreement.

Since the sleigh was still empty, all of us got to ride on it through town. Sitting in a sleigh, with the snow falling lightly falling all around us and the lights twinkling on all the houses and trees... this was the feeling of Christmas.

Chapter Eight

We all slept in the next morning as much as we could. But we could all hear Desi's excited footsteps as she ran up and down the hall. Getting up out of bed, I throw on my special outfit for the day. Since I was a child my family has always worn matching holiday themed pajamas all day on Christmas. It was normally a day filled with fun and relaxation with the family, so pajamas were worn the entire day. I loved it. Even though I was grown up and out of the house, it was still a small tradition I held onto.

After brushing my hair, I placed my sparkly blue and white headband on that matched the snowflake pattern on my outfit. I headed downstairs, joining everyone in the dining room. I noticed that for once, I wasn't the last one to arrive.

Mary had outdone herself this morning. Platters of

eggs, hash browns, bacon and toast, six different flavors of jams as well as three different types of juices, french toast and muffins covered every inch of the table. It smelled delicious.

"Dig in everyone," she said cheerfully. "Eat up, I've got plenty."

We all ate until we were stuffed. "I think I'm going to miss your cooking the most when I go home, Mary." I told her. I meant it too. There would be no one to cook amazing spreads like this for me at home.

Come to think of it, there wouldn't be anyone for me at all when I got home. It was going to be an entirely different situation. I wouldn't be going home to a loving husband. I would be going home alone, to a quiet and empty house.

"You alright there?" George leaned over and whispered. I snapped out of my sad thoughts. Today was supposed to be a happy day.

"Sure," I lied. "Just really full. Couldn't help it. Mary cooks too well," I winked.

"That she sure does," George agreed.

"I really ought to see if I could get some of her recipes before we leave here," Betty chimed in.

George smiled. "Everything you do is already perfect enough for me," he lovingly told his wife.

"Oh, George," she replied with a blush. Those two were so cute. I envied them. Envied their love.

Someday, I sighed.

We all helped clear the table and store the leftovers, even though there was barely anything left. "Come with me," Gabe told all of us. We followed him to the living room, to the tree we had all decorated the night before. It had a few gifts neatly wrapped and tucked under it. I hadn't thought about fake presents as decorations before. It was cute.

"First off, Merry Christmas!" he said.

"Merry Christmas!" Everyone returned. Hugs were given all around.

"Now, at the beginning of the week, we told you that here at the Snowfall Inn, we don't just consider you our guests. We consider you family. And to show you how much we appreciate all the help you've given us this week, we got you all a small present." he said as he gestured to the three. Desi let out a little squeal. "Now, they're not much, but it's something," he laughed.

"You didn't have to do that," George told him. "Just coming here and spending time with us was enough of a gift. We don't have any family nearby and it's not easy for us all to travel. You three always make us feel so at home. You have no idea how much that means to the two of us." He hugged his wife close and we all wiped away a tear.

Mary, Nicholas, and Gabe walked over and wrapped the older couple in hugs. It was such a sweet moment.

After everyone dried their tears our gifts were passed out. Betty and George received a beautiful antique box filled with recipes. "This is exactly what I wanted," George laughed loudly. "Thank you so much."

"I'll never be able to cook as well as you, Mary, but I'll surely give it a go. I appreciate it, really I do," Betty hugged the box tightly to her chest.

Tina opened a basket of self care items with a spa gift card, soothing face mask, bath bombs and the like, and also a bottle of local wine. "Every woman needs to be pampered," Mary said with a wink.

"I'm going to put each and every one of these items to good use," Tina assured her.

Desi was over the moon with her new wooden train set and stuffed snowman. "I saw how much fun you had making those," Mary pointed to the front yard. "So I quickly knitted you that little guy."

"You made that?" Tina asked, eyes wide. Mary nodded proudly. "We will keep it safe and treasure it. Thank you."

"It really was a fun day," Desi added, smiling up at me. I wrapped her in a quick hug.

"And this is for you," Nicholas said, handing me my box. The first thing I pulled out was a knitted snowman. "We match!" I told Desi, holding it up. The second and last item was a smaller box. I opened it up to find the most beautiful diamond necklace in the shape of a snowflake. My hand flew to my mouth.

"Gabe picked that out especially for you," he told

me, nodding to his son who was standing off to the side. I could see the hint of red in his cheeks.

"Thank you," I managed, barely above a whisper. "It's perfect."

"I saw it and immediately thought of you."

I laughed. "I do have an obsession with them. Thank you," I said again. Part of me wanted to run over and hug him, but I stayed put. I didn't know what Gabe and I were. Or what we could be. All I knew was what I wanted us to be. But it was too soon. Way too soon. Besides, I had no idea what his feelings towards me were.

Yummy food, drinks, and laughter flowed the rest of the day. It was an absolutely perfect Christmas. Everything and everyone was so relaxed. I was glad that I let my friends push me into coming still. It turned out to be exactly what I needed.

As the evening winded down I found myself letting a little sadness slip in again. Tomorrow morning I will be leaving this wonderful, magical place. It was always planned that way. Ethan and I were to spend the week leading up to Christmas day together for a wintery honeymoon, and then the next day head back to our normal everyday lives, to begin our married life together.

Gabe joined me near the fire as I sipped on my cocoa, the cup warming my hands. "Did you have a good Christmas?" he asked.

"The best," I lifted up the necklace that I had been wearing all day. I never wanted to take it off.

His smile was a little crooked, it was one of the sexiest things I've seen. "I'm glad. I know it's not what you expected it to be. But I'm happy to know that we made you smile even a little. No one should be feeling down at Christmas."

I nodded. I was feeling so many different things, all at once. So many emotions swirled around that I didn't trust myself to speak. Gabe must have picked up on that and together we just sat by the crackling fire, sipping cocoa and enjoying each other's company in silence.

After a while Gabe set his empty cup on a nearby table, clearing his throat. "Did you need a ride to the airport tomorrow? I would be more than happy to take you," he offered.

I swallowed thickly. This was a part I was dreading. "I was planning on riding over with Desi and Tina," I told him. Which was the truth, we were all leaving at the same time. "We have flights at just about the same time," I smiled. I didn't tell him that the real reason I didn't want him driving me there was that it would be too hard for me to say goodbye if it was just the two of us. That I was afraid to be alone with him because I just know I would say something stupid and ruin the magical week we just had. That I would tell him that I was pretty sure that I had started to fall for him. And my heart wasn't ready for that yet.

He just smiled like he understood. "At least you

won't have to wait at the airport alone," he let out a small laugh.

We sat for a bit longer, and when it got late, we said goodnight and headed off to our separate rooms.

For the first time since Ethan left me, I went to bed with tears in my eyes.

The next morning was fast and emotional. Everyone was trying to say goodbye to each other, with promises to call, write, and keep in touch. Desi had requested my address so she could write and draw me pictures, and also so we could make sure we both were taking good care of our snowmen.

I thanked everyone for their hospitality and for giving me the best holiday I've had in a really long time. I was sure going to miss them. Mary promised to mail me a few recipes so that I could work on my baking.

When it came time to say goodbye to Gabe all I could do was hug him. Again, I didn't trust myself to speak around him other than thanking him again for the necklace. After wiping away all our tears Desi, Tina and I headed off to the airport.

Chapter Nine

"Come on, Holly. You've been sulking around for weeks now. Let's go out and have some fun," Carol complained for like, the fifth time that day. She and Suzi have been bugging me daily to get out of the house and actually do something.

Ever since I came home from the Snowfall Inn I haven't been in the mood to party or anything like that. Most people just figured I was bummed out and feeling bad over Ethan, when in reality I missed the feeling I had on vacation. I missed the town, the people, and the festivities.

I missed Gabe.

He has been on my mind every second of every day since I left. I almost kicked myself for not asking him for his number when I left. Although, I wouldn't even know what to say to him if I did. I'm sure he's not even thinking about me. If Christmas time was any indication, he had a full, busy life down there. He certainly didn't have time to sit around pining for me.

Not that I was hoping he would be or anything.

"Please...." Suzi begged. "Just for a little while. We can go out, get some fresh air. It'll be good for you."

"I wanna go ice skating," Carol suggested. I can't remember the last time I went ice skating. I can remember falling down an awful lot though. Which is why I avoided that activity any way I could.

Suzi jumped up to go get her coat. "Excellent idea. What do you say, Hol?"

"I'm not any good at skating," I groaned. "Last time we went I walked away with a giant bruise." I grabbed one of the decorative pillows on the couch, trying my best to hide behind it.

Suzi laughed, yanking my fluffy shield away from me. "It'll be fun, I promise."

I doubt it. But to shut them up I grabbed my stuff and followed them to the local outdoor skating rink. Carol and Suzi both immediately strapped on a pair of skates and were effortlessly gliding across the ice. They made it look so easy.

I chose to stay on the bench, safely watching them from a distance. It did kinda feel good to be out in the fresh air, I'd have to admit. But there was no way in hell I was getting out on that ice.

Suzi and Carol skated over to me after a few minutes,

Carol on the phone. Suzi had the cheesiest looking grin plastered on her face. They were planning something embarrassing, I could just tell.

"What's up?" I asked, eyeing them both suspiciously.

"Look behind you," Carol said, putting her phone down. Suzi giggled.

I turned around and my heart stopped. There, standing directly behind me was Gabe.

"What? How did- You are-" I couldn't get a full sentence out, I was so surprised.

Gabe just smiled. "It took me a while, but I tracked down your friends and they helped me surprise you."

I turned to my two best friends, tears in my eyes. "You did this?"

Carol nodded. "Well, you've been such a mess ever since you got home. Even more so than when your ass of an ex broke your heart. So I contacted that Inn you kept talking about and put two and two together," she shrugged. "You're in love."

My eyes grew wide.

"It was so obvious," Suzi stated. "We've seen you in love before. This was a different type of sadness than basically being left at the altar. Oof," she said, as Carol elbowed her in the ribs. "Sorry," she squinted her eyes at me. "Poor choice of words."

"It's alright," I assured her. "But you two really did all this for me?"

"You know we would do anything for you," Carol

said, crushing me in a hug. "Besides, we were tired of you being a lump on the couch." I laughed as Suzi joined in the group hug.

I jumped back out of their embrace as I remembered that Gabe was standing there. "I'm sorry," I swiped at the tears in my eyes.

He waved off my words. "No need to be sorry. But I did have something to ask."

My heart skipped a few beats.

"I know we haven't spent all that much time together yet," he began. "But the time we did, felt amazing. It felt right being with you. When you left the Inn, I felt a part of myself leave right along with you. I missed you," he said.

"I missed you too, terribly." I admitted, feeling the tears prick at my eyes again.

Gabe took a step towards me. "I would like to spend a lot more time with you, to get to know you more. I don't want to be without you." He pulled a small box from his jacket. Suzi gasped behind me.

He opened the box, revealing a diamond snowflake shaped ring that perfectly matched the necklace that hung on my neck. I never did take it off. "Holly, would you be my girlfriend?" He asked, as the tears spilled from my eyes. This was the most romantic thing. "We may have to be long distance for a while, but I believe we can make it work. I want it to work. I want us to work."

"I do too," I nodded. "I would love nothing more than to be your girlfriend."

As Carol and Suzi cheered and hollered behind me, Gabe pulled me in and kissed me, wrapping his arms tightly around me.

I had never felt more at home and more loved than in this moment. I never wanted it to end.

About the Author

J.M. Goodrich is a native of Michigan's beautiful upper peninsula. She loves spending time outdoors as much as she can with her family when she's not reading or writing. She has been published in several different anthologies and novels of her own. She has written stories of romance, fantasy, and horror. In addition to her love of writing, she has a passion for music, and an obsession with The Beatles.